Desmonds
Birthday Party

Silver Dolphin

Ring, ring! went Desmond's alarm clock. "7 o'clock," he said. "It's time to get up! Today is the best day of the year. It's my birthday!"

Desmond bounded around his house, excited for his big birthday party. At 8 o'clock, he stopped for breakfast.

Can you find Desmond's biscuit sticker and add it to the picture?

"I need to buy lots and lots of things for my party," Desmond thought. "And I haven't got much time." At 9 o'clock, he rushed to the bus stop.

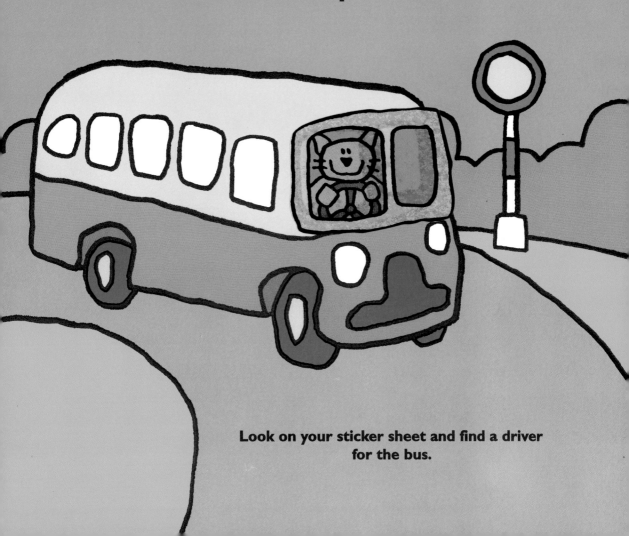

Look on your sticker sheet and find a driver for the bus.

Desmond's bus made 12 stops on the way to town.

Take your cardboard bus from the front pocket of this book. Move it along the roads to show how Desmond got to town. Start at 1 and finish at 12.

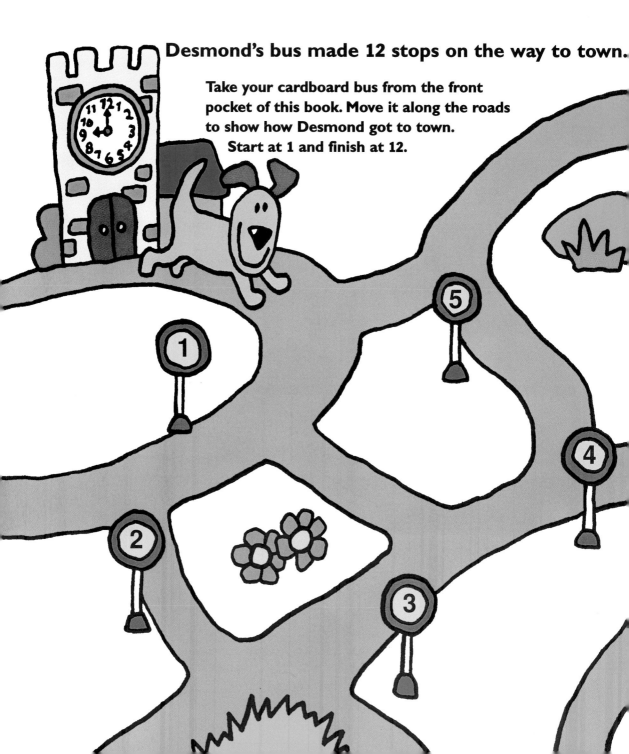

The bus took an hour to get to town. At 10 o'clock, Desmond walked into his favorite store. "Now, what do I need?" he asked himself. "Potato chips, drinks, and paper streamers!"

Find the can stickers and add them to the picture. How many cans of soda are there now?

Desmond was still at the store at 11 o'clock. "My bus doesn't leave until 12," he thought. "I have one hour to choose some fantastic party hats!"

Can you find another special hat and add it to the picture?

Desmond tried
on twelve different
party hats. You can
make one of these
hats at home. Ask
a grown-up to help.

1 Fold a large rectangle-shaped
piece of paper in half. Press it
down firmly.

4 Do the same to the other
corner. Make sure you press
the corners down firmly.

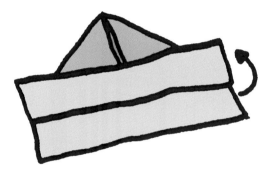

5 Fold up one side of the paper
at the bottom, as in
the picture.

2 Turn the paper around and fold it in half again to make a crease. Now open it back out.

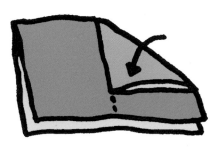

3 Fold down one corner of the paper so it meets the crease, as in the picture.

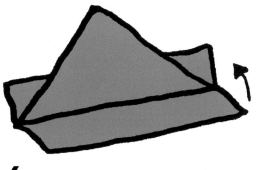

6 Turn it over and do the same to the other side.

7 Now you have a special hat that you can decorate, just like Desmond's!

**DONG! the big clock rang out.
Desmond counted the chimes:
1, 2, 3, 4, 5, 6, 7, 8, 9, 10, 11, 12.
"Oops! It's 12 o'clock already.
I'd better run for the bus!"**

The bus is waiting for Desmond. Add the bus sticker to your picture.

When Desmond got home it was 1 o'clock. "That means it's lunchtime," said Desmond. "I'll eat my lunch quickly, then make a giant birthday cake."

Find the clock face sticker that shows 1 o'clock and add it to the picture.

At 2 o'clock, the cake was ready to go in the oven. "I'll make some more food while it bakes," said Desmond. "Now, where is my cookie recipe?"

Add the cookbook sticker and some more eggs to the picture.

1 One cup of powdered sugar goes into the bowl first. Be careful not to sneeze!

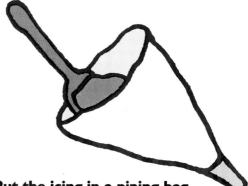

Desmond decorated some cookies to eat at the party. Ask a grown-up to help you make some icing for decorating.

4 Put the icing in a piping bag, and you're ready to decorate some round, flat cookies.

5 Add colored candy pieces and see how many designs you can make! Here are some that Desmond made.

2 Add some water to make the mixture a little runny. Just add a little at a time.

3 Add cocoa or a tiny bit of food coloring to the mixture to turn it a different color.

"It's 3 o'clock," said Desmond. "My cake is ready, and it looks delicious! Now it's time for the decorations. Where should I put all my balloons?"

Help Desmond to get ready by putting the cake sticker on the table.

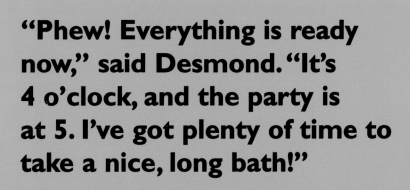

"Phew! Everything is ready now," said Desmond. "It's 4 o'clock, and the party is at 5. I've got plenty of time to take a nice, long bath!"

Can you find Desmond's rubber duck sticker and put it in the bathtub?

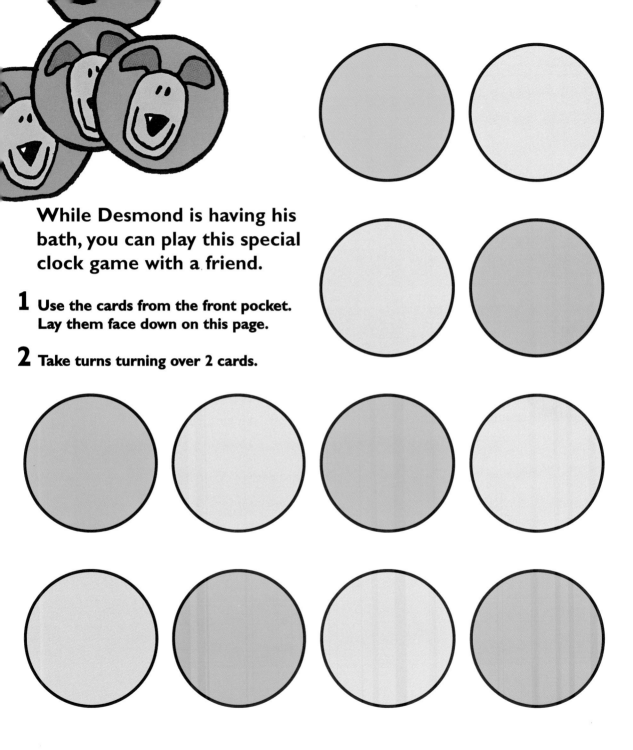

While Desmond is having his bath, you can play this special clock game with a friend.

1 Use the cards from the front pocket. Lay them face down on this page.

2 Take turns turning over 2 cards.

3 Say the time on the clocks out loud.
If the clocks match, keep them near you.
If they don't, turn them over again.
Play until you match up all the clocks.
The person with the most cards wins.

At last it was 5 o'clock. "Time for my party to begin!" said Desmond. His friends tumbled through the door shouting "Happy Birthday!"

**Find the clock face sticker that shows 5 o'clock
and add it to the picture.**

Desmond and his friends played games and ate loads of delicious food. Then it was time for Desmond to open his present. "It's a watch!" he exclaimed. "Now I'll always know the time. This is the best birthday I've ever had!"

Now make your own watch with t̶
cardboard pieces in the front poc̶

Silver Dolphin

Published by
Silver Dolphin Books,
An imprint of the Advantage Publishers Group
5880 Oberlin Drive, Suite 400
San Diego, CA 9121-4794
www.advantagebooksonline.com

© 1999 Design Eye Holdings Limited

Let's Start! is a trademark of Design Eye Holdings Limited

Story and pictures by Inc.

ISBN 1-57145-440-3

1 2 3 4 5 6 7 8 9 10 00 01 02 03 04

Manufactured in China